make a big difference to how well you do at school and to how successful you could be in life. literacytrust.org.uk

The Reading Agency inspires people of all ages and backgrounds to read for pleasure and empowerment. They run the Summer Reading Challenge in partnership with libraries; they also support reading groups in schools and libraries all year round. Find out more and join your local library: summerreadingchallenge.org.uk

World Book Day also facilitates fundraising for:

Book Aid International, an international book donation and library development charity. Every year, they provide one million books to libraries and schools in communities where children would otherwise have little or no opportunity to read: bookaid.org

Read for Good, who motivate children in schools to read for fun through its sponsored read, which thousands of schools run on World Book Day and throughout the year. The money raised provides new books and resident storytellers in all the children's hospitals in the UK. readforgood.org

*€1.50 in Ireland

Also by Frank Cottrell-Boyce

Millions

Framed

Cosmic

The Astounding Broccoli Boy

Sputnik's Guide to Life on Earth

Chitty Chitty Bang Bang Flies Again

Chitty Chitty Bang Bang and the Race Against Time

Chitty Chitty Bang Bang Over the Moon

the GREAT ROCKET ROBBERY

My name is . . . .

This World Book Day book is a gift from my
local bookseller and Macmillan Children's Books
#shareastory

To Lydia, future astronaut

First published 2019 by Macmillan Children's Books
an imprint of Pan Macmillan
20 New Wharf Road, London N1 9RR
Associated companies throughout the world
www.panmacmillan.com

ISBN 978-1-5290-1265-1

1 3 5 7 9 8 6 4 2

A CIP catalogue record for this book is available from the British Library.

Printed and bound by CPI Group (UK) Ltd, Croydon CR0 4YY

Holmen Paper and Gould Paper contributed towards the production
of this title printed on 52gsm Holmen Bulky

Frank Cottrell-Boyce

the GREAT ROCKET ROBBERY

Illustrated by
Steven Lenton

MACMILLAN CHILDREN'S BOOKS

The Dog Who Listens

I'm sorry if sometimes the words in this story come out wrong. I am not too used to words because I am a dog. Maybe you are asking yourself how come a dog knows how to read and also type using a computer. Well, there are many super-super-clever dogs. For instance:

- Chaser the dog, who can recognize nearly a thousand words of Human;

- Lada, who saved a baby whose human had left her behind in the supermarket and took her safely home in her pushchair;

• Jack, who saved humans from drowning in the Swansea River on twenty-seven separate occasions;

• And me . . . who wrote this book.

Maybe you are wondering how come a mere dog is able to do such super-super-clever things? For instance, me. This book will finally answer this question for all people for all time.

Like some dogs, I have my own human – namely an old man named Mr Mellors. He brings me food and water. He takes me on walks so I can meet other dogs, and he throws me things to fetch. If I poo in the wrong place, he clears it up.

Mr Mellors has a job – looking after me.

And I have a job – which is being a listening dog in the school library.

At my first day at St Francis Primary School, the librarian, Mrs Cotton, said to me, 'Barker –' (because that is my name) – 'we don't ask you to guard against burglars, or to herd sheep or to perform tricks. We just want you to *listen*. That's all. To listen quietly while the children read you stories. Good dog.'

Mr Mellors comes with me when I do my listening. He likes to listen too – mainly to stories about the sea, because once upon a time he was a sailor.

Some stories are hard for a dog to understand. Because the world seems different to dogs. For instance, dogs are close to the ground, so for them the world is mostly shoes, carpets and pavements. Also smells. So when a story says, '*The princess was fair of face*,' I want to say, 'How is that important? Who cares what her face is like? What does she *smell* like? Also, what shoes does she wear?' These are the things a dog needs to know.

But I don't say this. I only listen. Because I am a good listening dog.

By the way, that story turned out to be OK because the princess wore glass slippers. A human in glass footwear . . . For a dog, this raises an interesting and challenging question:

Can you chew on a glass slipper?

Some children think stories will be more interesting for me if they have dogs in them. NOT IF THE DOGS ARE NOT INTERESTING, THEY WON'T. For instance, *The Wizard of Oz*. This has a dog called Toto in it, and in the whole book, Toto does NOTHING. Except one time he chases a chicken. Also in Sherlock Holmes stories, there is a dog who doesn't do anything – not even bark!

Anyway, one day a girl came into the library smelling of sweets and school soap. Her name was Chelsea. She had a book with many pictures of dogs on the cover. Not boring dogs like Toto, or allegedly criminal dogs like the one in *The Hound of the Baskervilles*, but the famous hero dogs of rocket travel – Dezik, Zib, Belka, Strelka, Muschka – and the greatest Earth dog of all time, Laika. The book is called *Hero Dogs of Space*!

Hero Dogs of Space is the story of how, long ago, some scientists wanted to build rockets to send humans into space. But humans were scared that the rockets might not work, so they asked if some brave hero dogs would go up in the rockets first to see if they were safe. Because dogs are braver than humans.

At first, the dogs did not go all the way to space but just very high in rockets and then back down to the ground in parachutes. Alive! The terrible gravity and noise and speed of the rockets did not kill them.

Then came the greatest dog of all: Laika.

Laika was the first creature ever to successfully leave Earth. Her Sputnik rocket slipped through the atmosphere and out into space. She saw what no creature had seen before – the blue Earth twirling through the dark. All the world watched her. They took photographs. They made films about her. And a statue was built of her in Star City in Russia so that no one would forget that she was the first.

'Why would anyone,' said Chelsea, 'put a dog in a rocket? Dogs can't fly rockets.'

'Well,' said Mrs Cotton, 'they were using

Laika to see if the rocket was safe or not.'

'What happened to her?'

'She was never seen again.'

'Exactly,' said Chelsea. 'She probably crashed the rocket. Or took a wrong turn. That's what happens if you put a dog in charge of a rocket.'

Well, Chelsea, you are wrong! Laika did *not* crash or take a wrong turn.

The book *Hero Dogs of Space* is nearly all lies. For instance:

Lie Number One: It says that Laika was sent up in the rocket by humans to see if space was safe.

Not true! Laika was not sent up in a rocket like some kind of space parcel. She took that rocket and flew it herself, because she wanted to go to space. Afterwards humans pretended they had sent her because they were embarrassed to admit that a dog had stolen their rocket.

Lie Number Two: Laika was never seen again.

This is a lie because . . . LAIKA LIVES!

Yes – Laika survived.

So here it is . . .

The True Story of Laika (including an explanation as to why some dogs are super-super-clever – for instance, me).

The Dog Who Went For a Swim

In Russia, in Freezing Cold City, almost none of the dogs have humans to take care of them. Freezing Cold City is called Freezing Cold City because it's freezing cold. The wind might turn your tail into one big icicle. The small dogs of Freezing Cold City live on the streets. They know all the tiny, warm corners of the city, the shop doorways and the alleyways. They know how to get humans to give them food by doing tricks or being friendly.

But the two most important things they know are:

1. Small Dogs stick together.

2. Small Dogs avoid the Man with the Head Shaped like an Egg.

The Man with the Head Shaped like an Egg puts tempting food in warm places. They know not to touch that food. That food is a trap. The Man with the Head Shaped like an Egg will appear from the shadows and stuff you into his sack. He will take you away, and you will never see your dog-friends again.

One small dog who knew all these things was Laika.

She knew which bins had the best food. She knew the many warm places by the docks where the big ships sailed into the town's port through the ice, carrying timber and fish.

In the daytime, she stuck together with her friends – a company of small dogs called the Company of Small Dogs.

One night, Laika was settling down to sleep under a pile of sacks on the edge of the dock when she heard a big splash.

Next, she heard barking.

She looked out from under her sack and saw a small red dog, with a foxy face, splashing about in the freezing cold sea. Laika rushed down the steps to the water's edge to help. She barked at the little red dog to swim over to her, but the little red dog was sinking.

There was a huge great timber ship in the dock and, floating behind it, tied to a post on the dock steps, was a little rowing boat. Laika leaped into the rowing boat and bounded to its prow. 'Come here!' she barked across the freezing water. 'I will help you climb aboard.'

She could see that the little red dog's feet were tied together with rope. Some horrid human had got bored of looking after her and had thrown her into the water to drown. Sometimes there are bad humans who don't look after animals faithfully. One thing Laika had learned about humans was this:

Humans = Unpredictable

All at once, the air was filled with the smell of peppery sausage and engine oil. And then – even more unexpectedly – the rowing boat suddenly began to move. Laika looked behind her. A young sailor with a neat beard had jumped aboard and was rowing the boat out to the middle of the dock. He got alongside the drowning dog, pulled her out of the water, and dropped her into the boat.

The little red dog was saved!

Did the little red dog say, 'Thank you for saving my life, I was so scared!'?

No.

The little red dog said, 'That was fun! But now I am absolutely starving. Can you recommend somewhere to eat?'

Laika was shocked by her bad manners, but the sailor did not understand what the little dog was saying. He only heard her happy barking. He took a towel from his kit bag to keep the little red dog warm and dry. But before he could wrap her in it, the little red dog shook herself dry. Water from her wet fur sprayed all over everywhere, including over the young sailor and Laika.

This is where the sailor throws the dog back in the water, thought Laika.

But no. He only laughed.

'We just saved you from drowning,' said Laika, 'and now you're nearly drowning us with your wet shakes!'

'I was not drowning,' said the little red dog. 'I was swimming. A brisk swim is my favourite way to start the day, though it does always make me starving hungry. My name is Krasavka, by the way.'

'And I'm Laika,' said Laika. 'Do you always go swimming with your legs tied together with rope?'

'Ah,' said Krasavka.

'Shall I untie you?'

'If you don't mind . . .'

Laika had learned to untie knots while she was living on the streets. She had learned many things there. 'If you lie on your side, it'll be easier.'

The young sailor kept talking, but the dogs didn't understand a word he was saying because they didn't speak Human. Also, he didn't understand anything they were saying to each other because he didn't speak Dog.

Laika was worried when she saw him take out a knife. But he used it first to cut Krasavka free, then to cut a chunk of peppery meat from a big sausage wrapped in paper, which he kept in his pocket. He fed this to the dogs, which was a treat.

'Just what I needed,' said Krasavka. 'I love humans. Don't you love humans? The way they bring you food, throw you things to fetch, and if you poo, they clear it up after you.'

'Or possibly tie you up and throw you in the dock?' said Laika.

'Exactly. What a great joke. Humans! They're all about the fun!'

Laika was beginning to wonder if the shock of the cold water might have messed up the workings of Krasavka's brain.

This was a question that was answered a few

seconds later when Krasavka said, 'Well! Must be getting home!' and tried to climb out of the boat and walk on the water.

'Whoah!' said Laika, pulling Krasavka back on board by the scruff of her neck.

'Silly me,' said Krasavka. 'Forgot about the freezing water. I'll go home when we are on dry land. It'll be easier.'

'Krasavka,' Laika said. 'The city is a dangerous place at night. Get some sleep, and we will see what tomorrow brings.'

'Good idea,' said Krasavka. And with that, she turned around three times (dogs do this to shake off the cares of the day), lay down in the bottom of the boat, and went straight to sleep.

'You can't just sleep in someone's boat,' barked Laika gently in her ear.

But when the sailor saw Krasavka snoring, he just laughed again, took off his coat, and laid it over her. He seemed happy for Krasavka to sleep there.

He seems, thought Laika, *to be the kindest person I have ever met.*

The sailor leaned back in the boat, looked up at the stars, and began to tell Laika all about them. He pointed out the brightest star in the sky and told her how the people of the South Pacific used it to navigate the mighty ocean. And how the Ancient Egyptians had cheered every year when it rose in the night sky, because it meant that the River Nile would flood and make the land fertile. He said he loved that star because he knew it was going to show his captain the way back home. He thought she would be interested because – as you know – the brightest star in the sky is called the Dog Star.

But he said all this in Human, so Laika didn't understand a word.

Except . . . Laika learned something new. Which was:

If you really listen, you don't have to understand the words to understand what a person is saying.

Laika listened to the happy-sad tune of the sailor's voice and decided to try her best to learn to understand Human. Already, she understood that he was talking about home. She had never had a home, but the tune of his voice told her that home was far away, and that he wanted take her there; that home was a place where a person would be welcomed and warmed and would never have to worry ever again about the Man with the Head Shaped like an Egg.

Laika was exactly right about what home is like. But she got the address completely wrong. She somehow got the idea that the sailor was telling her that her home was on the Dog Star, and that he was offering to take her there on his ship.

We all make mistakes.

The sailor had a medal around his neck on a chain. He took it off and hung it around Laika's neck instead. He told her it was an award for bravery; for saving the other dog's life. He also told her that the man whose picture was on the medal would look after her wherever she went. He said all this in Human too, so she didn't understand that either. But she did understand his laughter, and she liked the chinking of the chain because it sounded like laughter too.

Maybe it was the gentle rocking of the rowing boat, maybe it was feeling safe because a kindly human was near, but soon Laika fell into a deep, warm sleep in the sailor's lap.

When Laika woke up the next morning, the sailor was gone.

Not just the sailor, but his ship too!

All that was left was the laughing jingle of his chain as she turned her head from side to side. And the faint smell of smoked sausage from the piece of newspaper lying in the bottom of the boat.

Laika's heart howled with sadness. In the far distance, she could see a smudge of smoke from a ship disappearing over the horizon. For a wild moment, she thought maybe she would try to swim after it. But then Krasavka woke up.

'That was a mighty sleep. The only trouble with a really mighty sleep is that it leaves you STARVING hungry. Shall we go home and get breakfast?'

'I don't have a home,' said Laika. 'And the humans at your home threw you in the water with your legs tied together.'

'Not that home,' said Krasavka. 'The home in my dream. Where it's warm and safe and the sailor with the neat beard takes care of us, just like on your medal.'

Laika couldn't see her medal. But Krasavka was right. It showed a man with a beard – who looked a little bit like the sailor – gently holding the paw of a wolf.

'I dreamed all about him last night. Didn't you?'

Laika was amazed. Until then, she hadn't remembered her dream. Now it came back to her in full colour. (Well, in blue and yellow, as these are the only colours dogs can see.) It was exactly the same dream as Krasavka's. Except in *her* dream, it was not just Laika and Krasavka who had gone there and been welcomed at the gate by the sailor – it was the whole Company of Small Dogs from Freezing Cold City.

But how could two people have the same dream?

Laika had a thought about dreams:

A dream dreamed by one person is just a dream. A dream that you can share is a quest.

Something in the corner of Laika's eye fluttered in the breeze. It was the newspaper the sausage had been wrapped in. On the front page was a photograph of a rocket flying through the stars. Laika was sure the sailor had left it behind on purpose to show her how to get home. She decided there and then that she would find a rocket and fly home to the Dog Star. Her heart tightened with the hugeness of her notion.

'Krasavka,' she said, 'we are going on a quest.'

'What,' said Krasavka, 'is for breakfast?'

The Dog Who Ate the Pies

SUMMER

The quest that Laika wanted to share was to lead the Company of Small Dogs out of Freezing Cold City towards their true home in the stars.

Krasavka's quest was . . . breakfast.

The two dogs headed into the city: one in search of a new world; the other in search of a juicy bone.

If you are a dog, the main sights of Freezing Cold City are boots tramping by very fast in a hurry, pavements covered with half-melted snow, and the smell of seagulls and fish guts.

Does this sound grim?

It was not grim for Laika, because Laika was on a quest. And here is what Laika had learned about quests:

When you are on a quest, every step that takes you nearer to your goal is glorious. Even if you're stepping through fish guts.

Krasavka felt that way too. 'What a great city!' she cried. 'Here's a lamp post that smells strongly of dog wee. Let's wee our reply.'

Dogs, as you know, communicate mostly through wee.

Laika realized that Krasavka could not read dog wee very well.

'This wee,' she explained, 'says, "*I am a massive and ferocious dog. Any small dog found weeing near my lamppost will be eaten – by me – with a blunt spoon.*"'

'I see,' said Krasavka. 'Maybe let's wee somewhere else then.'

'I know just the place,' said Laika.

In the middle of Freezing Cold City stands a huge statue of a woman wearing a woolly hat, a big fur coat, big woolly mittens, and big heavy boots. She is so wrapped up in coats and scarves, you can't see her face. The statue is called *Summer in Freezing Cold City*. In the pavement round the back of the statue is a warm-air vent from the Underground Railway. This is the entrance to the secret headquarters of the Company of Small Dogs. Every time a train goes by, deep beneath the pavement, a whoosh of hot air gushes up through the vent and swaddles you in diesely warmth.

Laika brought Krasavka there, then howled a good-morning howl. Soon two, three, four and then more than four small dogs turned up. (This is how dogs count, by the way: one, two, three, four; more than four; many more than four; many, many more than four; much more than four; much, much more than four . . . and so on.)

The dogs greeted each other in the usual

way – by sniffing each other's bottoms. Then Laika introduced them all to Krasavka, and they all sniffed her bottom politely. Their names were Belka, Strelka, Dezik, Muschka and their leader, Zib.

Zib invited Krasavka to join the Company.

'Krasavka,' he said, 'now that we have all sniffed your bottom, we all agree that you are invited to join the Company of Small Dogs. We stick together. We help each other. We watch out for the Man with the Head Shaped like an Egg.'

'Actually,' said Laika, who was bursting to tell the others about her quest, 'we have come to ask YOU to join US in a great enterprise. A quest!'

Before she could finish, Belka said, 'Laika has a chain around her neck.' Belka was always the first to notice things. And the last to let you finish your sentences. 'Does that mean,' she said, 'that you've found a home?'

The only dogs in the city that had chains or collars around their necks were dogs who were cared for by humans.

'It's a picture of a man with a beard stroking a dog,' said Belka.

'That must be my sailor!' said Laika. 'He lives in a place where dogs will always be safe and warm and he will be their human. Tell them about our quest, Krasavka.'

'We are on a quest,' said Krasavka, 'for breakfast.'

Real cold – the kind of cold they have in Freezing Cold City – does make you hungry, so as soon as Krasavka said 'breakfast', the whole Company of Small Dogs forgot everything except the possibility of breakfast.

The Company of Small Dogs has two main food sources. One is the food that humans throw away – in bins or round the back of shops and cafes. The other is the food they beg for from humans.

'I can do that,' said Krasavka. 'I know all about humans. I used to live with them.'

'It's more complicated than it sounds,' said Laika. 'We have studied humans carefully.

The bigger your eyes are, the more they like you.'

'That's me,' said Krasavka, whose eyes really were very large.

'Best thing is if you can do tricks. Humans love tricks. They always reward a trick.'

'Tricks?' said Krasavka.

'Like this,' said Muschka, getting up and walking around on her back legs like a human. Muschka was famous all over Freezing Cold City as the Dog Who Could Walk on Her Hind Legs. When she did her trick, humans handed over their lunch. Simple.

Krasavka said she knew an excellent trick and couldn't wait to show it off to the others. So, they took her to the tram station. There were always plenty of humans there, often eating while they waited for their tram. When they arrived, they spotted a family sitting on a bench at a distant tram stop, laughing and joking and eating hot pies from the hot-pie stall.

The Company of Small Dogs watched from

the other side of the road as Krasavka strolled over to the family. They waited to see what special trick she would do. First, she nuzzled up to the smallest child in the family, then suddenly she gobbled the child's pie whole. The child howled and pointed at Krasavka. The Company of Small Dogs watched in horror. During the confusion, Krasavka pounced on the next child's pie and swallowed that whole too.

'What. Is. She. Doing!?' gasped Laika.

'She's destroying the Company of Small Dogs' reputation for good manners and entertainment value,' said Zib.

The father and mother leaped to their feet. The mother poked Krasavka with her umbrella. The father kicked her with his big boot.

'Small dogs stick together,' said Laika. 'We've got to go and save her.'

Just then, the eldest child, a boy, picked up Krasavka by the back legs, whirled her around, and flung her across the road.

She landed with a thud at Laika's feet.

'Are you OK?' asked Laika.

'Humans are such fun!' whimpered Krasavka. 'Did you see that boy dancing with me?'

'No – but I do see an entire family running towards us waving their umbrellas angrily!' said Laika. 'Run!'

'Oh!' whooped Krasavka. 'Hide-and-seek! I love it!'

The dogs tore off down alleys and side streets with the family in hot pursuit. They jumped on to a passing tram and rode it for three stops until the conductor threw them off. Soon the pie-less family were out of sight. They were probably too hungry to keep running.

'Your new friend,' said Zib to Laika, 'is a problem.'

Laika was just about to answer when Krasavka gave a yelp of joy.

'Look!' she said, pointing urgently with her nose.

There – high above their heads – was a big, bright, yellow star.

'We've found our home!'

The Dog Who Ate the Sausages

The star was made of glass and tin, lit by electricity, and screwed to the wall above the door of a butcher's shop. There was writing around the outside of the star. They couldn't read it though, because in those days, dogs could not read.

But just so you know, it said:

> *Pole Star Butchers*
> **Pleased to meet you**
> **Meat to please you**

Is this is it? thought Laika. *Is this really the star I'm searching for?*

This star seemed a lot bigger than the one the sailor had pointed to. Maybe it was because they were nearer to it, now that they had gone three stops on a tram.

'Come on in,' said Krasavka. 'There's plenty of food. Just like in our dream.'

'This is a butcher's shop,' said Zib. 'If we go in there, they will send for the Man with the Head Shaped like an Egg, and we will all be bagged and taken away.'

Even as he said this, the other members of the Company of Small Dogs were staring in at the window, where strings of plump sausages were cuddling up to haunches of beef on great beds of juicy bones. They knew that what Zib said was true. But the sight of all that meat was turning their jaws to water and their brains to jelly. After all, they had just watched Krasavka eat a whole pie. That's got to make a dog feel hungry.

'You know,' said Belka, 'I've never seen the Man with the Head Shaped like an Egg in real life. Maybe he's just a story.'

'The butcher isn't in,' said Dezik. 'Maybe he's gone on holiday. In which case, it would be very wrong to leave all that meat.'

'Here's the door – look,' said Krasavka. 'A small door in a big door, because it's for Small Dogs in a Big City.'

Every one of the Company of Small Dogs knew that the small door in the big door was really for the butcher's cat. He kept her to frighten away the mice. But plump sausages and juicy bones were working melty magic on their hungry dog brains.

'You would fit through there easily,' said Krasavka to Dezik. 'You're the smallest dog here.'

'I'm bigger than you,' said Dezik. 'You're tiny.'

'That's only on the outside,' explained Krasavka. 'I'm actually part husky and part wolf. I'm huge on the inside.'

Considering he was a dog, Dezik was unusually interested in handles and buttons, in things you could pull and things you could press. So he slid through the cat flap and investigated the locks and handles of the butcher's front door. In seconds, it was open. The smell of meat rushed out of the shop like an excited mother welcoming home her children. It wrapped them in its delicious embrace and pulled the Small Dogs inside.

The Small Dogs did not eat everything in sight right away.

Oh no.

At first, it was just the bones. *Sometimes the butcher throws us bones*, they thought. *Maybe he won't mind if we take these ones.* They jumped on to the counter, taking care to tread softly when they walked across the meat. They even wiped their paws so as not to get the meat too dirty.

You didn't have to eat sausages to enjoy them; you could drape them round your neck to make the other dogs laugh. You could lounge on them like cushions while you sucked on a juicy bone. That's what Muschka did, to amuse everyone. She honestly did not plan to eat any sausages . . . not at first.

Meanwhile, Dezik had spotted a handle that looked like it would enjoy being pulled. It was attached to a big metal machine at the back of the shop. There were diagrams screwed to the side of the machine. The more Dezik looked at those diagrams, the more he was sure they meant something. The more he thought about what that meaning could be, the more he was convinced that they meant extra sausages.

This is the moment that Dezik came up with Dezik's Theory, which nowadays all puppies have to learn.

Dezik's Theory states:

If a button is pressed or a lever is pulled in one place, something will happen in a different place.

He pulled the handle. The machine shuddered. Its insides churned like a hungry giant's stomach. A hole like a mouth opened in its side, and a new sausage slid out. Then another

. . . and another. Sausage after sausage. A cascade of sausages snaked on to the counter. So many sausages, it would be rude not to eat them. Surely they HAD to eat them to stop the shop filling up with sausages? Surely when the butcher came back, he would be DELIGHTED that they had eaten them?

The door opened.

The butcher looked in.

The butcher was NOT delighted.

Small dogs are not humans, but they can often tell what a human is feeling. Especially if that human is waving a meat cleaver while running straight at them.

Laika knew nothing about the sausage chaos in the butcher's shop. As she was about to go into the shop with the others, she noticed something on the floor – a piece of old newspaper with a photograph of the same rocket she'd seen on the sailor's sausagey newspaper in his boat. When she looked down at it, the chain around her neck had jingled merrily. It had reminded her of the sailor's laugh . . . When she eventually looked up again, she glimpsed the Dog Star shining high above the roofs of the houses. She felt that it was waving down at her, telling her to hurry up.

Then Dezik shouted, 'Hurry up! We'll all be killed!'

And she saw the flash of a meat cleaver out of the corner of her eye – and she ran.

The Last Dog in Town

The Company of Small Dogs had been chased by angry humans before. So they knew what to do. They all ran off in different directions and met back at their secret headquarters.

'Small Dogs,' said Zib gravely, when he had made sure they were all back in one piece, 'we are in big trouble. First there was the stealing of the family's pies; then there was the invasion of the butcher's shop. Humans will be angry with dogs. They will not let us shelter in their doorways any more. They will stop giving us food in exchange for tricks. They will chase us with meat cleavers and throw cold water on us when we aren't looking.'

The other small dogs snarled at Krasavka. 'You've ruined everything,' they said in unison.

'But, Small Dogs,' said Laika, 'do not despair. Freezing Cold City is just a place. Krasavka and I are going to lead you to a new home where the sailor with the beard will be our human, and there will always be food, and you will feel lighter than air.'

'It's going to be like a big party,' said Krasavka.

'Where is it?' said Muschka.

'It's among the stars. All we need is a rocket.'

'A rocket!' Dezik gasped. 'It's hard enough to get a human to give a dog a bone. What human would give a dog a rocket?'

'I've been all over this city,' said Belka. 'There are no rockets here. Where will you find a rocket?'

'I don't know,' said Laika. 'That's why this is a quest.'

Everyone looked at Zib to see what he would say.

'Life was always hard in Freezing Cold City.' Zib sighed. 'Now, thanks to Krasavka, it will be even harder. A rocket sounds impossible. But maybe life in Freezing Cold City will be impossible too. I think we should go on this quest. Follow Laika.'

With a nod, Laika began to lead the way on their expedition, but they had barely quested a couple of hundred yards when Krasavka asked, 'Are we there yet?'

'Surely you should know,' said Zib. 'It's your home we are travelling to.'

Another hundred yards further down the road, Krasavka said, 'I'm starving. This questing is a hungrifying business.'

'We've barely begun!' said Dezik.

Across the road was a street lamp, and steaming temptingly in a pool of yellow street-lamp light was a bowl of chopped meat with a side order of dog biscuits. Laika saw it, so did Zib and the other Small Dogs. They said nothing because they had also seen, etched on the side of the bowl, the egg-shaped badge of the Man with the Head Shaped like an Egg. They knew it was a trap. The dogs shuddered and hurried on.

All except Krasavka, who was already way behind. She called to them, 'Small Dogs, look! Breakfast!' And before they could stop her, she had dashed across the road.

Laika almost shouted, 'Stop, Krasavka!' But for one fatal second, she thought, *This quest would be a lot easier without her always going on about food*.

Then for another fatal second, she thought, *Maybe Muschka is right, and the Man with the Head Shaped like an Egg is just a story*.

For a third fatal second, she – and all the other Small Dogs – thought, *Until Krasavka came along, life was all right in Freezing Cold City*.

In those three fatal seconds, something round and shiny appeared in the lamp light. It was a head shaped like an egg. Krasavka barely had time to yelp a warning. The Man with the Head Shaped like an Egg picked her up and stuffed her into his sack.

'No!' Laika howled and charged after him. Maybe she could bite the sack open and rescue Krasavka.

But by the time she had caught up with him, he had thrown the sack into a trailer attached to the back of a motorbike. He turned his egg-shaped head towards Laika. He grabbed her by the scruff of the neck, stared at her with his egg-shaped eyes, then suddenly dropped her and kicked her away from the van.

In case you're wondering, the man with the egg-shaped head was wearing a crash helmet. He had egg-shaped eyes because he also wore goggles. He pushed Laika aside because he saw she was wearing something around her neck and thought that meant she belonged to someone. He only took dogs with no owners. So the medal had saved her.

The sailor saved me, she thought.

As she picked herself up off the pavement, Laika's first thought was, *So, the Man With the Head Shaped like an Egg is real after all.* Then she turned around and saw the most terrifying thing she had ever seen: more Men with Heads Shaped like Eggs. Four more, more than four more, many more than much more than four – all stuffing small dogs into sacks and throwing them on to trailers. Then they got on their motorbikes and zoomed away, and Laika was left all alone.

She was the last Small Dog in Freezing Cold City.

The Dog Who Caught the Train

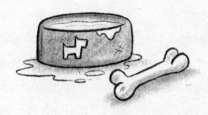

Laika was at a crossroads. One road led down to the docks. If she went that way, she could find a boat and set sail. The other lead towards the Even Colder Mountains, which lay beyond Freezing Cold City. She could see the motorbikes carrying her friends off down that road. She could try and rescue them, or she could follow her quest towards the stars.

Here is what Laika realized just then:

If your friends need you, but you turn away from them, then you will be lost.

'Small Dogs must stick together!' she panted to herself, chasing after the motorbikes without a clue what she would do if she ever caught up with them.

Laika was fast. Not as fast as a motorbike, but then she didn't get stuck at traffic lights or behind big, slow bin lorries. She hurtled across crossroads and through underpasses. Whenever she lost sight of the motorbikes, she opened her nostrils and tried to catch a whiff of the biscuity smell of Krasavka on the morning air.

Laika was running out of breath.

The motorbikes were not running out of petrol.

But they did stop.

Laika watched the egg-headed men climb off them. They slung the wriggling sacks of dogs over their shoulders and strolled into a huge building made of stone and glass. From somewhere beyond the building came the loud screech of a steam whistle.

Of course!

The station!

The dogs had all been loaded on to a train.

Laika hurtled on to the platform just as the stationmaster waved his flag. The last door slammed. The train rolled forward on its mighty wheels. Laika launched herself at the back of the train, through clouds of steam. When the steam cleared, she found herself clinging to a buffer just a few feet above the track. She clung there all day and all night, and then the whole of the next day too, as the train hurtled on oblivious. It was not as hard as you might think – the air was so cold, it had frozen her paws to the metal.

But the day after that, the train left all the snow behind and began thundering through the desert. The sun beat down on the metal of the handrail until it became too hot to touch. It heated the chain around Laika's neck until it was fire at her throat. It blasted the sands of the desert so that they shimmered like smoke.

At a bend in the railway where the train slowed down, Laika finally let go and tumbled on to the sand. By the time she had scrambled back to her feet, the train had disappeared into the distance.

Alone, under the hot sun, Laika thought, *I've made a terrible mistake. Of course dogs don't live in space! Krasavka is an idiot. I have let a dream dreamed by an idiot lead the whole Company of Small Dogs to its destruction!*

With these despairing thoughts weighing down on her heart, Laika walked until she came to a little wooden station. She slid into its shade and turned around three times and slept.

When she woke up, someone had left a bowl of water and a juicy bone next to her. There was no sign of any human. The bone was wrapped in newspaper. On the front was the photograph of the rocket again. She was sure that somehow the sailor had sent these things.

She guzzled the water and sucked on the bone. No human came. But night came, with its cloak full of stars. They were so much brighter and more beautiful than they had been in town. Surely they must be nearer too. So even though Laika had abandoned her original quest to try to save Krasavka, she somehow seemed nearer to the end of her quest just the same. It was as if Krasavka, who had been wrong about almost everything else, had actually been right about this.

So this is another thing Laika learned about quests:

It doesn't matter if you stop believing. Just keep moving, and help will come.

The Dog Who Lost the Rocket

The next day – refreshed and full of hope – Laika trotted along the railway line, sure she was heading in the right direction. But when evening fell, her spirits fell too. The track passed through a huge great pair of metal gates, too high for any dog to climb, too heavy for any dog to open. A metal fence stretched into the distance, to the left and to the right. The gates must have opened for the train then closed again after it had passed through.

This was the end of the line.

For a long time, Laika stared at the signs on the gate. She felt sure that they told you how to open the gates. She felt sure that life would be easier if she could just speak human. She decided then to listen hard any time a human spoke. Then she did what any dog – and most humans – would do at a time like this. A nice long wee on the fence. A wee that said simply, *I am here. Where are you?*

Soon the breeze brought the smell of an answering wee. But this was not a wee she had ever smelt before – it was pungent, acidic and frightening. She looked around. Ragged shapes were silhouetted against the desert moon. They moved swiftly and silently before her, their shadows shivering like flags.

She could hear slavering jaws.

Smell the breath of hunger.

See wicked green eyes glitter.

. . . *Wolves.*

She backed up against the gate, hoping against hope that it would open.

And it did.

'Laika! I could smell your wee. I thought it might be just a dream!'

It was Krasavka!

There was no time to wonder how Krasavka had got there, or how the Dog Who Was Wrong about Everything had arrived in just the right place at just the right time.

All Laika had time to say was, 'Krasavka! Wolves! You said you were part wolf. Maybe they are your cousins. Please tell them to leave me alone.'

Krasavka took one look at those green glittering eyes and said, 'I may have been mixed up about that. I don't think I *am* part wolf. I think I'm entirely a very Small Dog. Run!'

They ran through the gate and across the moonlit roads beyond. The wolves howled and chased after them. Sand flew around their feet like ghosts.

'We are doomed,' said Krasavka.

The ground began to shake. Could that be the wolves? The wolves were many and fierce, but they weren't exactly heavy. Why would the ground shake? The air rumbled. Rumbled, not howled. It was not a wolf-like noise. Something huge and terrible was happening. But what?

The wolves did not wait to find out. They fled.

The sky blazed briefly, bright as day.

And, at last, Laika saw it blasting into the sky.

Her rocket.

She had found her rocket.

But just . . .

Too late.

It was already a thousand feet out of reach and climbing.

The Dog Who Let the Dogs Out

'Don't be sad,' said Krasavka. 'We have found home. Look . . .'

She nodded up at the sky. The stars seemed so close, walking felt like flying. Krasavka lead Laika to the back door of a little house. Two children came running out to stroke her and tickle her tummy.

'See?' said Krasavka, showing Laika that she had a collar around her neck. 'I have a home! A family of humans. The grown-ups feed me. The children play with me. I live in a warm house now.'

Soon they heard the deep, cheerful voice of the children's father.

Laika held her breath, wondering, *Could this be the sailor?*

No. This man didn't even have a beard.

But he was good. He looked at the medal round Laika's neck, then nodded his head, and the children cheered. Once again, the sailor's medal had taken care of her. It had convinced the man that Laika belonged to someone. She could stay until that someone found her.

'When we arrived, the humans looked at all the dogs on the train, and these humans picked me,' said Krasavka, preening a little.

'What happened to all the other dogs?' asked Laika.

'Oh, I'm sure they're all fine,' said Krasavka. 'The humans here are so kind. Welcome to Unbelievably Hot Town.'

Laika did not need to turn around three times when she climbed into her basket, because nothing was troubling her. She listened to the voices of the children. She was sure they were speaking to each other, just like dogs speak to each other. If she just listened hard enough, she might begin to understand. But then, not far away, she heard a different sound – dogs yelping. On the night air, she smelt something she had not smelt since Freezing Cold City.

Fear.

Somewhere nearby, Small Dogs were afraid.

Laika woke Krasavka. 'Are you sure the other Small Dogs are happy like you?'

'Nearly sure.' Krasavka shrugged. 'Go back to sleep.'

'Small Dogs,' said Laika, 'stick together.'

And with that, Laika got out of her basket and followed the scent of fear out into the night.

The sun was coming up. The sky was growing lighter. Silhouetted against it, Laika saw something that made her stop in her tracks. Rockets. More than four of them. A thicket of rockets. Unbelievably Hot Town was the place where nearly all the rockets in the world were being built at that time. By trying to rescue her friends, Laika had somehow arrived in the very best place on Earth to steal a rocket. This was another thing she had learned:

**If you do the right thing, you will
end up in the right place.**

Following their scent, she found the other dogs in a long, low building. The door was not locked. It didn't need to be.

Because inside the long low building were cages. The walls were lined with them. Cages upon cages upon cages. Inside every cage was a dog. Every Small Dog from the Company of Small Dogs was locked in a separate cage. When they saw Laika, some of the dogs yelped to be let out. Others were too weary and sad even to yelp. Some were too big to move inside their cages.

It was a dog prison.

The Dog Who Stole the Rocket

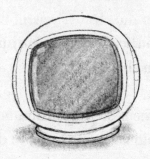

You can read about what was happening to those dogs in *Hero Dogs of Space*, because I admit that particular chapter is not all lies, unlike the rest of the book. All day, the space scientists whirled the dogs around in machines to test their resistance to gravity. They put them in fridges to see if they could stand the cold. They put them in heated glass rooms to see if they could stand the heat. They taught them to press certain buttons by giving them electric shocks when they pressed the wrong ones and a treat when they pressed the right one. They covered them in wires and connected those wires to machines so they could measure the dogs' heartbeats and brain patterns.

Hero Dogs of Space is right too about what the scientists did. But it was not right about why. That book says the scientists wanted to send the dogs into space.

Of course they didn't!

They thought dogs were dim.

Why would they put a dog in charge of an expensive rocket?

They were using the dogs just to experiment and test things. To make sure it was safe before sending a human up in a rocket.

The scientists had paid the Men with Heads Shaped like Eggs to catch dogs from the streets for this experiment because they thought that if the experiment went wrong, no one would mind. Because no one would miss a dog from the street.

They were wrong about this. Laika missed them. And now she had found them, she was going to save them.

'Small Dogs,' said Laika. 'Life in Freezing Cold City was very hard for us. Then you came here, and it became harder again – with cages and electric shocks. Life is not meant to be hard. It is meant to be good, with warm blankets, juicy bones and people and dogs being kind to each other. If life is hard, that must mean we are in the wrong place. Our right place is in the stars. And now here is the rocket that will take us there.'

Zib was the first to laugh.

Then all the other dogs laughed.

'Ridiculous,' said Zib. 'Who would put a dog in charge of a rocket?'

'We knew we needed a rocket,' said Laika, 'and now here we are right next to one. Even though we never tried to find it. We have been brought here for this purpose.'

'To go to space,' explained Dezik, 'you need a special space suit. Go through to the next room, and you will see the space suits hanging up. Ask yourself, are they dog-shaped?'

In the next room, Laika found a row of space suits – with helmets attached – hanging from a row of clothes pegs. They all looked human. In fact, they all looked like the Man with a Head Shaped like an Egg.

'Then we won't wait for the humans to send us,' she said when she went back to the other dogs. 'We will just take the rocket.'

'That would be stealing,' said Zib. 'Look how bad things got when we stole meat from the butcher. Stealing rockets is probably worse.'

'But would it be stealing?' said Muschka. 'Sometimes a human throws a stick away. We run and get it for him. Then what? They throw it away again. As for the rockets, they build them, then they blast them off into space. If you ask me, they don't know what they want.'

Laika wasn't really listening. Laika was staring out of the window at the rocket. Its pointy nose seemed to be yearning to fly. Its finny tail made it look like it was standing on tip-toe. She was so busy being in awe of the rocket, she didn't notice that two scientists had walked into the room. They talked a lot in

Human. One of them stroked her head. They probably discussed whether she should be in a cage and probably decided no because of the medal round her neck.

She had an idea. Sometimes she had looked at a pie in a certain way, and the human had felt sorry for her and given her the pie. Maybe this would work with a rocket. She looked longingly at the rocket. One of the humans burst out laughing. Then the other did the same. She knew they thought the whole idea of a dog in a rocket was funny. And she knew that for the sake of all dog kind, she had to show them that it wasn't funny.

It was going to happen.

'Small Dogs,' she said, 'we are going steal a rocket.'

'We can't,' cried the dogs. 'We're stuck in these cages.'

'Dezik's Theory states that if a button is pressed or a lever is pulled in one place, something will happen in a different place,' said Dezik. 'There's a lever next to the door.'

As soon as the humans had gone, Laika pulled the lever.

All the cage doors opened.

'Good theory,' said Laika.

'I have another theory,' said Dezik. 'That it's impossible for a dog to fly a rocket.'

'And I have my own theory,' said Laika. 'And it's this . . .'

Impossible things are just a lot of possible things put together in a different order than usual.

'Who,' she said, 'will come to the stars with me?'

'Whenever you mention the stars,' said Zib, 'it makes me think of that butcher's shop in Freezing Cold City. The one with all the sausages.'

'Me too,' said all other dogs, one by one.

'An impossible rocket,' said Zib, 'is a beautiful dream, but a sausage is a sausage.'

So the Company of Small Dogs decided

to take the train back to Freezing Cold City. But before that, they would help Laika to fly, because Small Dogs stick together.

It's easier than you think for a dog to steal a rocket.

The first problem was to get past the guards who were watching the rocket.

Muschka had a plan for that. 'As you know,' she said, 'I love tricks, and I can walk on two legs. If two dogs got inside one of the human space suits – one in the head, and one in the legs – then the one in the legs could walk on two legs, and together they would look like a human in a space suit.'

Dezik volunteered to be the walking dog. 'I am very interested in levers and buttons,' he said. 'I have a feeling that the rocket is full of them. I would like to see inside it.'

Muschka gave Dezik a walking lesson. The two dogs climbed into their space suit and strolled past security.

Laika's heart beat fast as they climbed the

steps to the tip of the rocket. One guard did stop them and ask them a question, but Laika pointed to her helmet as if to say, '*I can't hear you*.'

And there she was – at last – standing in the doorway of the rocket.

'Wait,' said Dezik. 'Controls. Where are the controls?'

Laika looked around the steely clean interior of the rocket. There was not one single button or lever.

'How do we make it take off, then?' asked Laika.

'We can't,' said Dezik. But then he slapped his head. 'Of course! What is Dezik's Theory?'

Laika closed her eyes and recited, 'If a button is pressed or a lever is pulled in one place, something will happen in a different place.'

'So if you want something to happen in one place,' said Dezik, 'go and look in a different place! See you later!'

And with that, he disappeared.

Alone now, Laika stepped into the rocket, not knowing what might happen.

The first thing that happened was that another dog turned up.

'Krasavka!' Laika gasped. 'You can't come! You've already found your home.'

'It's warm and friendly,' said Krasavka, 'but it's not home.'

'But they care for you and . . .'

'I really wanted my human to have a beard like the one on your medal. Every time I look at this one's chin, I feel disappointed. Also, in my dream, home was more floaty.'

'Floaty? What does that even mean?'

But before she could answer, a voice came over the radio. '*Dezik to Sputnik*,' said the voice.

'Who on earth is Sputnik?' asked Laika.

'It's the name on the side of your rocket,' said Dezik. 'I found the button-and-lever room. There are helpful diagrams. Button up your space suit, I'll pull some levers, and we'll see what happens.'

Dezik pulled a lever. There was the sound of running water. Because he'd pulled the flush of the toilet. Next he pressed a button.

The rest is history.

Dezik had sent the first Earth creatures into space.

Laika and Krasavka.

The Great Rocket Robbery was complete!

The Dog Who Told This Story

The history book *Hero Dogs of Space* says that humans used dogs to test their rockets. Humans told the story like this because they were embarrassed to admit that Laika STOLE their rocket. A mere dog was the first to conquer space, not a human.

Since then, humans have followed dogs into space. So I don't need to tell you all about the deafening roar of the engines and the incredible squashing gravity that made Laika and Krasavka feel like they were being flattened. Or the gorgeous moment when the gravity changed, and they felt themselves begin to drift weightlessly through the air like a pair of helium balloons.

Krasavka whooped. 'I told you it would be floaty! I wonder if it is because we haven't had breakfast. Is there any food?'

Laika didn't answer. Through the window, she could see Earth, thousands of miles below her, turning in the darkness, as though it was a blue jewel resting on a black hand. No living creature had seen it from this far away before.

She realized that all the blue was sea. Planet Earth was nearly all sea. She thought about her sailor, sailing back and forth across the ocean. Her necklace jingled like a laugh, and she thought, *I have made a terrible mistake. Of course the sailor is on the sea, not in space. And now I'm in space, and he's on the sea, and I'll never see him again—*

Just then there was a knock at the rocket door.

Impossible! you say.

You should know by now that impossible things are always happening.

Laika stared at the door. Could it be the

sailor? Could he be outside ready to come in and find her?

She looked at Krasavka. 'Who could it be?' she said, hardly daring to hope.

'Pizza delivery?' suggested Krasavka.

Who was at the door?

Aliens.

The aliens didn't need to open the door. They passed through the metal the way light comes through a window. Then, like sunbeams, they hovered all around the dogs.

I can't describe what they looked like any better than this because there are no human words for what they looked like. The dog words are:

Yeeeeoooyipyipfrrrrrr

If that's any use.

The aliens were friendly.

The first one through the door said, 'Cool rocket. Did you build it yourself?'

'Not entirely,' said Laika.

'Are you from that little blue planet down there?'

'Yes. But not the blue bit.'

'We really want to go and visit, but it looks really wet. Is it worth visiting?'

'Oh yes, oh very, yes,' said Laika.

'Maybe you could be our tour guides?' suggested the alien.

So that's what happened. Laika and Krasavka were taken from their tiny Sputnik rocket up on to the vast alien spaceship where they gave illustrated talks about life on Earth. The aliens could change their shape with a single thought. When they finally visited Earth, they went disguised as dogs.

'Definitely go as dogs,' said Krasavka. 'Dogs are the best.'

'I like the look of the human shape,' said the alien.

'Humans bring you food,' said Krasavka. 'They save you from drowning, throw sticks for you to fetch, and if you poo in the wrong place, they clean up after you. Dogs have all the fun. The planet belongs to dogs.'

From then on, the aliens that came to visit Earth did so disguised as dogs.

So when you come across a dog who can recognize a thousand words of Human, or who brings a baby home from a supermarket, or saves people from drowning, it's probably not a dog. It's probably an alien having a holiday on Earth.

But not if a dog writes a book.

Because I wrote this book, and I actually *am* a dog. A dog that learned to understand Human. A dog that learned to write. You're wondering how? Read on . . .

The aliens wanted to thank Laika for her help. She asked them if they could help her find the man whose picture was on the medal around her neck. So they went to Earth and searched for him. The good news is that it was really easy to find him because he was super-famous. The bad news is that he wasn't her sailor.

'The man on your medal isn't your sailor,' one alien said, 'because the man on your medal has been dead since the year 1226, because that's a medal of St. Francis, the patron saint of animals.'

'But he can't be!' said Laika. 'He's been looking after me! How could he do that if he's dead?'

'We can't really go into detail,' said another alien, 'but the fact is that the universe is stranger than you think. In fact it's stranger than anyone can think.'

Laika's eyes grew so big with disappointment that the aliens agreed to help her find the good sailor with the neat beard. It wasn't easy because most sailors are good, especially the ones with neat beards.

Then one day, the first alien found a sailor with a neat beard who lived in Scotland, and the sailor had named his house Laika. Could that be him?

They took Laika down there and left her on the doorstep.

And the rest is not history.

But it is true.

Why did the sailor name his house Laika? Because years before, he had known a little Russian dog who barked a lot (she was trying to talk to him). '*Laika*' is Russian for 'Barker'.

And how do I know all this?

Because I am the dog that knocked on the door.

Don't believe me? Look at my human's nice neat beard. Look at the chain around my neck.

Are you wondering how Laika can still be alive after all these years? On Earth, dog years are shorter than human years. In space, it's the other way around.

You see, the universe really *is* stranger than anyone can think.

THE END

IF YOU ENJOYED THE GREAT ROCKET
ROBBERY, YOU MIGHT ENJOY STORM HOUND
BY CLAIRE FAYERS – READ ON FOR A TASTER!

*'Myths, legends, stories.
They are all words for facts that
people have forgotten.'*

Storm of Odin is the youngest stormhound of the Wild Hunt and he can't *wait* to haunt the lightning-filled skies with his fearsome howls. But on his very first hunt, Storm finds he can't keep up and falls to earth, landing on a road outside Abergavenny, Wales.

Enter twelve-year-old Jessica Price, who adopts a cute puppy from the rescue centre. And, suddenly, a number of strange people seem very interested in her and her new pet, Storm. People who seem to know a lot about magic . . .

Discover a legendary tail of magic, myth and a *very* unusual dog from the author of The Accidental Pirates series and *Mirror Magic*.

He was Storm of Odin, last-born hound of the Wild Hunt that runs across the plains of the sky on stormy nights. He was barely four months old, but almost as tall as the crimson-tailed horses that raced before him. His coat was the black of the deepest midnight, his eyes shone golden-bright, alive with excitement.

He was Storm of Odin and this was his first hunt. He opened his mouth and howled, his voice joining the cries of the pack around him. The scream of hunting horns echoed between the wide horizons, and moonlight glanced off the hunters' helmets and the tips of their spears. Sky and earth trembled together.

He was Storm of Odin, and . . .

. . . he was having a little trouble keeping up.

He ran as fast as ever – faster, in fact, because he was straining now, his muscles beginning to ache, and the wild joy of the hunt was being overtaken by an uneasy feeling that all was not well. He dropped his head and his howls became a series of pants and grunts as he struggled to keep his legs moving forward. The crimson horse-tails were no longer in his face but flickered in the darkness ahead.

The stormhound slowed, and his paws began to sink through the cloud beneath him. He howled again, his voice less like thunder across cloud-topped mountains and more a cry of 'Hey, wait for me!'

No one heard. No one waited.

The Wild Hunt rushed on.

Far behind them all, Storm of Odin uttered a final yelp and fell from the sky.

Morning came and brought a headache with it. The sunlight made everything bright and sharp-edged – much bigger than he'd expected. The sky, no longer thunder-filled, was a clear, light grey, speckled with white wisps that didn't deserve the name of clouds. Mountains rose in indistinct humps all around while, closer by, trees towered over him, their branches hung with faded green leaves. Grass pricked at his paws as he took his first step.

Where was he?

The only creatures in sight were a huddle of sheep staring at him from a field on the other side of a grey stripe on the ground. A road – he'd heard the huntsmen speak of them. Humans built them because they didn't have wild horses to carry them. Instead, they crawled along these grey paths in armoured shells like snails.

The stormhound stepped on to the road to look about. The surface was rough, surprisingly hard, and smelled of warm stones and tar. A large sign stood opposite.

Y Fenni 5
Abergavenny 5

These shapes meant nothing to him. And why weren't the sheep fleeing from him in terror, or falling at his feet in awe? Were they so stupid they didn't know who he was?

'Hey! Sheep!' the stormhound shouted.

The sheep gazed blankly at him, chewing grass. Eventually, one of them wandered closer. *You talking to us?*

Who else I would I be talking to? A growl rose in Storm of Odin's throat as he prowled forward. *I am Storm of Odin of the Wild Hunt. Did you not hear us pass by last night?*

The sheep looked at one another and back at him. *If you're a stormhound*, said the one who'd spoken before, *I'm Aries. The Ram – get it?*

And I'm Rameses of Egypt, another one baaed. The whole flock fell about laughing.

Storm of Odin growled again in annoyance. *You're not even rams, you stupid sheep.*

The sheep only laughed harder.

Caaaaaaar! one of them shouted.

The stormhound shook his head. *Don't you mean 'baaaaa'?*

The ground trembled. Storm of Odin leaped backwards just in time. A rush of air, a noise like thunder and something metal roared by on the road. It was vast – the size of a chariot, and almost as loud as the Wild Hunt.

A moment later it was gone.

The stormhound rolled over and came up coughing. The air tasted of smoke and oil.

Car, the sheep said smugly. The rest of the flock chewed grass frantically, looking as if they were trying not to laugh.

Another of the metal things rushed into sight and shot by, faster and noisier than anything the stormhound had seen in his short life.

What do you get if you cross a stormhound and a sheep? one of the sheep asked. *A very baaaaaaad dog. Go back to the sky, storm puppy. It's not safe here.*

Storm puppy? Storm of Odin growled at the insult. He put a paw on the road, intending to cross over and teach the sheep a lesson, but he felt another rumble begin to build and stepped back. Odin would smite the sheep for their insolence when the Hunt returned. He turned his back on the sheep with as much dignity as he could muster and began to walk.

He was much slower than last night. The thorny weeds at the side of the road stung his paws and every time a metal car came past, the wind buffeted him and he had to flatten himself to the ground. After a while, rain began to fall and he plodded on through puddles. He wanted to sit down and rest but forced himself on. This grey road must lead somewhere – why else would the humans rush along it in such a hurry?

Then, unexpectedly, a car swerved to the side of the road and stopped. A door opened in the side and a man stepped out.

Storm of Odin began to growl and stopped in surprise. The man was huge; so tall, his face was a faraway blur. The stormhound scuttled backwards on his bottom. This was far worse than he'd thought. He hadn't fallen into the world of men, after all, but a land of giants!

The giant squatted and stretched out a hand, palm down. 'It's all right.'

No, it wasn't all right. It was very *not* all right. The human world was not supposed to be this big.

Unless . . .

Oh no.

The thought had been knocking quietly for his attention for some time, but Storm of Odin hadn't wanted to let it in. Now, it overwhelmed him. He looked down at the earth, at his two front paws, glossy black and quite small in the grass. He felt one of his ears flop sideways and though he growled with effort, he couldn't make it stand up again.

The man was not a giant. Storm of Odin was small. This world had shrunk him. He let out a whimper of despair.

The man lifted him out of the grass with hands that smelled of mint and soap. Storm of Odin bared his teeth.

'You're a fierce little thing, aren't you?' the man said, and ruffled the stormhound's black ears.

This was worse humiliation that anything so far. When the great Lord Odin got to hear about this he would smite this man and his tin shell from the face of the earth.

'What kind of person would abandon a puppy?' the man asked.

The Wild Hunt, that's who. But it wasn't their fault I got left behind, and they'll be back soon, so if you will kindly release me and be on your way I will consider asking Odin not to blast your home and family with thundery vengeance.

The man clearly didn't understand a word. Instead of putting Storm of Odin down on the ground, he carried him to the metal shell and placed him gently on the back seat. Then he produced a blanket and proceeded to dry the stormhound's wet coat.

A fluffy blanket. Pink, printed all over with

kittens and smelling of cat.

This was too much. Storm of Odin shook himself free and stood up, ready to enact his own thundery vengeance here and now, but the man had already let him go and was climbing into the front seat of the metal shell.

'Hold tight, little guy,' he said.

Little guy? Eat lightning, human!

The metal shell rumbled and lurched. The stormhound's stomach lurched with it. On second thoughts, he'd just lie here and chew the man's blanket for a while. That'd teach him.

About the Author

Frank Cottrell-Boyce is an award-winning author and screenwriter. *Millions*, his debut children's novel, won the CILIP Carnegie Medal. His books have been shortlisted for a multitude of prizes, including the Guardian Children's Fiction Prize, the Whitbread Children's Fiction Award (now the Costa Book Award), the Roald Dahl Funny Prize and the Blue Peter Book Award.

Frank is a judge for the BBC Radio 2 500 Words competition and, along with Danny Boyle, devised the Opening Ceremony for the London 2012 Olympics. He lives on Merseyside with his family.

About the Illustrator

Steven Lenton is based in Brighton and loves to illustrate books, filling them with charming, fun characters that really capture children's imaginations. As well as illustrating Frank Cottrell-Boyce's multi-award winning books, he is the illustrator of the bestselling and award-winning Shifty McGifty and Slippery Sam series. Steven also illustrates the Nothing To See Here Hotel series, the first of which won the Sainsbury's Children's Fiction Book Award 2018.

StevenLenton.com

DESTINATION:

ADVENTURE!

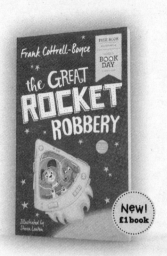

A world of possibilities

the NOT-SO-GREAT Train robbery

the Perfect crime
–IT'S A WORK OF ART

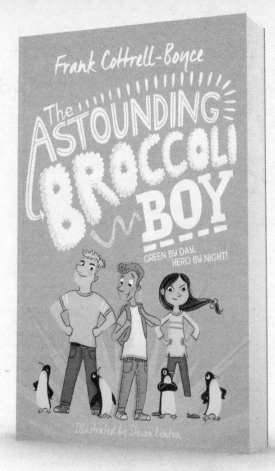

GREEN BY DAY,
HERO BY NIGHT!

WORLD BOOK DAY

SHARE A STORY

From breakfast to bedtime, there's always time to discover and share stories together. You can . . .

1 TAKE A TRIP to your LOCAL BOOKSHOP

Brimming with brilliant books and helpful booksellers to share awesome reading recommendations, you can also enjoy booky events with your favourite authors and illustrators.

 FIND YOUR LOCAL BOOKSHOP: booksellers.org.uk/ bookshopsearch

2 JOIN your LOCAL LIBRARY

That wonderful place where the hugest selection of books you could ever want to read awaits – and you can borrow them for FREE! Plus expert advice and fantastic free family reading events.

 FIND YOUR LOCAL LIBRARY: www.gov.uk/local-library-services/

3 CHECK OUT the WORLD BOOK DAY WEBSITE

Looking for reading tips, advice and inspiration? There is so much for you to discover at **worldbookday.com**, packed with fun activities, games, downloads, podcasts, videos, competitions and all the latest new books galore.

SPONSORED BY

NATIONAL BOOK tokens

Celebrate stories. Love reading.

Well **hello** there! We are

Overjoyed that you have **joined our celebration** of

Reading **books** and **sharing stories**, because we

Love bringing **books** to you.

Did you know, we are a **charity** dedicated to celebrating the

Brilliance of **reading for pleasure** for everyone, everywhere?

Our mission is to help you discover **brand new stories** and

Open your mind to exciting **new worlds** and **characters**, from

Kings and **queens** to **wizards** and **pirates** to **animals** and **adventurers** and so many more. We couldn't

Do it without all the amazing **authors** and **illustrators**, **booksellers** and **bookshops**, **publishers**, **schools** and **libraries** out there –

And most importantly, we couldn't do it all without …

YOU!

On your bookmarks, get set, READ! Happy Reading. Happy World Book Day.